Red, White and Black

Red, White and Black

Emma Ferraro

Believer's Dream Publishing

www.believersdreampublishing.com

The text of this book is set in 12-point Trebuchet MS
Printed in the United States of America

ISBN: 978-0-9832273-5-9

First edition

First printing, July 2014

For Carys,
Thanks

Chapter 1

"No, over there! That one is so Red!" Marilyn was pointing to a pinstriped fedora in the window of a trendy-looking store. I had to agree, it was very me.

I'm Raquel Reeves. But everyone calls me Red. Why? Well, I'm albino, so of course one of my trademark features is my pigment-lacking eyes. I guess it must be the only way people can remember my name—I'm not very popular and pretty introverted. I don't like bothering the few friends I have with tons of whiny complaints. It's just not who I am.

The few friends I have are close, though, and they're kind of awesome. I've known Marilyn since the third grade. We do pretty much everything together and she gets me, but doesn't take any sass. I like that; it keeps me from spontaneously transforming into a hormone-driven teenage girl every five minutes.

Here, strolling at a leisurely pace through the sketchy community mall, Marilyn and I were searching for my "new identity." We rushed into the store, and in two seconds she had thrown the fedora onto my head.

"Ooh! Mirror! Look in it! See? What did I tell you?" I turned around and located the mirror on the wall behind me. To my surprise, I did look rather saucy in this hat that seemed to have been made for me. It should have looked awkward against my translucent skin, but it didn't. I looked hot. Because this feeling has always been rare for me, I shut my gaping mouth, shrugged, took off the hat, and got in line to pay for it.

A content smile was spreading across my face when I noticed that Marilyn was stroking my new hair feather.

"It looks really pretty," she assured me. I had to admit that it honestly did. As I thanked her for convincing (forcing) me to get the red-and-black striped one installed a little over an hour ago, I secretly envied how utterly perfect the teal feather looked against her curly brown hair. "By the end of today, you'll be a totally new Red!"

Yeah, about the whole reinvention thing. I never really had amazing luck with guys. Actually, I was picked on as a kid because I was different. My worst experience was a guy I liked in middle school calling me an "ugly ghost." It pretty much made me hate myself for an entire year. But freshman year, I had my eye on a guy who was popular, kind of a jock (I think he played baseball or something), and soon I was head-over-heels. I could swear I was dreaming when he asked me out. But I wasn't. He held my hand in the hallway for a few weeks; then he started to kiss me before each class. I was beginning to think that love was possible for me to reach. Those dreams were shattered, however, when I heard in study hall that he was back together with his ex. Sure enough, there they were, making out next to the bathrooms before first period. The only thing he had to say: "You worked great. Hey, thanks!" At least he thanked me.

I shut down after that. After crying myself to sleep for months (okay, so I ran out of tears after about two weeks), I came to the conclusion that my demeanor was to blame. People thought I was, for lack of a better word, soft, because of my pale skin and simple clothes. It was time for a change.

Now it was August, the day before the start of my sophomore year and a new, edgy Red would soon be walking those halls. No one else would ever mess with my heart and I would never again set it out to be taken.

Upon closing the front door, twenty shopping bags and a backpack in tow, the expected happened.

"And where on earth have you been?" My mother does this every week.

"With Marilyn; it's Tuesday," I reminded her.

"You didn't text me saying you'd be late!"

"Check your phone," I said, plopping my bags down next to the stairs. I made my way over to the kitchen, where she had been furiously scrubbing the stovetop.

"Oh, heh heh, never mind," she finally replied, checking the fifty texts she had forgotten to check throughout the day. "What did you get at the mall?"

"Lots of really cute stuff," I showed her the fedora with a grin and a twirl.

"Ooh, very nice! And I like your hair!"

"Thank you!" I said, stroking my feather. "I'll just go put all this away." I grabbed my multitude of purchases and trudged up the stairs.

The next couple of hours were spent gleefully unloading the pieces to my reinvention and laying them out for me to wear the first week of school. Punk-chic jacket after rebellious boots after saucy fedora reminded me of the person I was going to be this year. And it made me excited. No more tears, no more mushy disposition. I was determined to throw romance to the wind and focus on me, for I was convinced that if vulnerability meant inevitable destruction, what was the use of taking that risk?

As I crammed a jacket-laden hanger into my closet, I could hear my mother shout my name from the kitchen. It was time for dinner. I took one last look around my room and soaked in the satisfaction of my scheme, then flipped the lights off and bounced downstairs.

"Pass the salt?" I blurted through a mouthful of somewhat bland potatoes. My mother slid the shaker across the table into my hand.

"Would it kill you to chew with your mouth closed?" She teased with a snicker. I gave a sarcastically playful smile and shoved another forkful into my mouth, ever the graceful lady she raised me to be. There was a gap of silence; then she asked, "You know Mrs. Leighton from my office?"

"Yeah?" I replied.

"Well... she has a son about your age-"

Oh geez.

"We were talking today and you kids came up, and I told her about your... unsuccessful relationships-"

"Mom!"

"We decided to plan something for the two of you," she stated bluntly as she dug her fork into a stray green bean.

"Uh... like a date?"

"Yes, at Arlecchino's, Saturday night at seven. We made reservations."

I was dumbfounded. Speechless. How was I supposed to live up to my new tough exterior with these plans set in motion? Besides, my mom and I aren't totally distant, but she doesn't exactly know the kind of guy I would go for. How did this evening, the last one before the start of a new school year, turn so horrible so quickly? The only thing I could think to do was to push my chair away from the table and head bitterly up to my room.

"His name is Finn! He goes to Roxdale Charter!" she called after me.

"Whatever."

Chapter 2

I slammed my locker door even harder than I do after a bio exam.

"Can you believe it?" I half-asked, half-shrieked at Marilyn.

"Whoa, whoa, whoa. So you've never even met him, he's a guy your mom picked out, and you're having dinner with him at some fancy-shmancy restaurant on Saturday?"

"Yeah, and he goes to Roxdale Charter."

"Nub," she snarled. "Hey, cheer up. It's one night, and it cannot be that bad."

"That's not what I'm worried about. After what happened last year, just talking to a guy doesn't feel right."

"He's not Jake!" Marilyn knew more than anyone else how imperative it was that no "Jake" ever found his grimy way into my life again. When I spent weeks crying my eyes out after my last go at romance, it was Marilyn who dropped everything and showed up at my doorstep with a tub of Rocky Road, ready for a marathon of Girl Code. When I lost sight of who I was and where I wanted to go, boy-related or not, it was always

Marilyn who pointed me on my way, probably making a joke every now and then to get me to laugh and hold my head up. At the end of the day, I knew in my heart that she would always have my best intentions in mind. "Red, you need to do something for yourself. I know it's not ideal, but it's the first day of a new year. It's time to have a little fun."

"Fine," I agreed, "I'll try." And with that, we were off to health.

I was intently watching Cassie summon her father's dark magic when the T.V. shut off, abruptly ending my Secret Circle marathon.

"Mom!" I complained. "It's Saturday! That's my T.V. day!"

"You've been sitting there watching all day. It's 5:30! Get off that couch, hop in the shower, and get all gussied up! We're leaving at twenty to seven."

With a groan, I managed to pull myself up and start the shower. Forty minutes later, I was downstairs in jeans and a nice sweater. The look on my mother's face said, "Now, now, you can try a little harder." My guess was pretty close.

"You finally meet a nice boy and you don't even try!"

"But I haven't met him!"

"Well, not looking like that!"

Soon enough, she had me with my hair in a bun, and in a conservative black dress that said, "I'm looking to get into law school, not into your pants." But she had done my makeup, and I looked pretty cute. Well, with the eyeliner, I looked like a True Blood character, but it was good enough.

We arrived at Arlecchino's, a nicer restaurant downtown, at about five to seven. The atmosphere was sophisticated and refined, a smidgen too much for my taste. I hesitated upon entry, but mom made her way right up to the young hostess.

"Reservation for Leighton-Reeves, seven o'clock," she said as if she had done it a million times, which she probably had. My mother used to go on dates all the time; my father left her as soon as she told him she was expecting. Honestly, I've never really had any desire to find him, or even know who he was. Although at times, I must admit I've found myself wishing I had known him, just long enough to let him shape my life. Instead, as a child I relied solely on my mother, who decided a few years ago that love would come when it came, and has since thrown herself into work.

The hostess ran her perfectly manicured fingertip down her little list. When her finger stopped and tapped on a name, she looked up with a large, fake smile and said, "Right this way, your party is already waiting."

As she gestured for me to follow her, I could hear my mother say under her breath, "Such a gentleman!" She then called out, "Call me when you're almost done."

"Kay," I agreed as I followed Sally Sunshine.

"Love you, have fun!" And with that, she blew me a kiss and left.

We made our way through the maze of fancy tables seated with young lovers and well-off families. Out of the corner of my eye, I spotted a quaint elderly couple feasting on gourmet-looking raviolis, staring deep into each other's eyes. A sort of sentimental feeling flushed over me as I realized the true extent of a lifelong love. I realized that one day soon, one of these starry-eyed lovers would die peacefully in their sleep, and the other would go on loving them, loving them and cherishing them until their own time came, pushing the boundaries of this cliché, timeless emotion. Upon glancing away from the adorable couple, my gaze met that of a young teenage boy, about my age. He was skinny, but his sleeves were rolled up enough to expose a little tricep.

"Here we are," said the hostess. My heart skipped a beat. This must be Finn. "Your server will be with you shortly." And she left us there, just the two of us.

Once I sat down, I got a closer look at him. He wasn't strikingly handsome or anything, maybe even a little goofy looking. He looked like the kind of guy I'd be friends with, though. He—Finn—had curly brown hair, was pretty pale- like me, only not quite to the same extent- and had brown eyes that seemed friendly, maybe even a little nervous. Over a dress shirt, he sported a sweater vest. Yes, a sweater vest. What else could you expect from a Roxdale Charter student? If this were to progress, and I wasn't sure there was a huge possibility of that happening, it probably wouldn't work out. Roxdale kids apparently have a ton of homework, so he might not have time for me. Why would he make time for me?

He smiled and reached his hand across the table. "Hey. I'm Finn. Nice to meet you."

Chapter 3

"Hey," I stammered, forcing a smile. I reached my hand across the table to shake his. Was it too late to back out? I couldn't help but think that this was a bad idea. Finn's hand was reassuring, though, and I realized that he must feel exactly the same way.

"You must be Raquel."

"Call me Red," I requested through pursed lips. Since the third grade, my mother has been the only one to refer to me by my name. When Finn said it, I couldn't help but think of her talking about me behind my back.

"Red, huh? That's interesting," he said, but not in a condescending way.

I nodded, and he looked around casually.

"This is... really awkward, isn't it?" I pointed out.

"Yeah. I've never really done this blind date sort of thing. And to top it off, my mom made me wear this stupid sweater vest!"

Oh, thank God that wasn't his move.

"But you, you look great," he complimented. And I giggled. Come to think of it, no guy I'd been with had ever told me that I looked nice. It made me feel... special.

"So you go to Roxdale?" I asked.

This started a sufficient conversation about our schools, homework, the people at them, our friends. Finn was surprisingly easy to talk to. Then a thought crossed my mind.

"Oh, I haven't even looked at the menu!"

"Right! That might be a good idea."

My eyes glazed over the menu, passing items that I probably couldn't pronounce even if I lived at Arlecchino's. But something did catch my eye.

"Cheesecake!" I exclaimed in a whisper.

"Really? Where?"

I realized how totally classy I sounded. "Oh, I mean, I don't want to be rude. I could get it later... for dessert..."

"No! I love cheesecake! You know, I'm not really all that hungry. Wanna just split a cheesecake?"

Slightly embarrassed, I agreed. About then, our waiter, who had brought us our Dr. Peppers while we were talking (we were practically taste bud twins), came and took our order. We spent another hour or so talking and sharing one exquisite cheesecake. It even tasted expensive. I brought up how I'm in school newspaper and want to major in journalism. It turned out that he wrote songs and poems. We were both writers. Finn was also a musician; he taught himself to play drums and piano, only he didn't make a big deal out of it. I hadn't checked the time once until I finally felt my phone buzz in my purse.

"Let me know when you're almost ready," was what my mom had texted me. I closed out of the text and saw that the time on my phone read almost nine o'clock.

"Wow, it's nine already?" I asked in disbelief.

"Whoa, is it really? Guess time flies when you're having fun!"

And it was true. I had completely let down all my walls for Finn. He was funny, warm, and easy to talk to. I wasn't even trying. It all just came... naturally. As if he was already a good friend.

We paid for our food with the money our parents had given us, I replied to my mom's text, and we started saying our goodbyes.

"Red, I honestly didn't expect to have fun tonight. But, hey, you're really cool."

"Hey, thanks, you too." I hadn't brought up the subject all night, but when you're me, this kind of thing is inevitable. "And Finn... you don't mind... the way I look? My skin? My eyes?"

"You're so unique. And I'm not saying that just to avoid an awkward conversation or to be nice or anything. You're flawless. You have no idea how hard it is to come across a girl who's so pretty, yet so smart and awesome to talk to."

This changed everything I thought I knew about guys.

"And I think we should do this again," he added. "Well, maybe something a little more comfortable."

We each put a five on the table as a tip and got up from where we had spent our whole night lost in each other's company.

"Yeah, that would be really cool," I said.

"Is that a yes?" He put his arms out in a shrugging gesture. I took the opportunity to give him a goodbye hug.

"It's a hopefully."

Chapter 4

With Sunday came boredom. Marilyn was on some church retreat, but she still made sure to text me every so often. Our conversation went like this:

Marilyn: Sooo how was the date?
Me: It was actually okay. Tell you more tomorrow.
Marilyn: Sounds good. The guy next to me smells like beef jerky.

The rest of the day I reflected on what had happened. I really did have fun. I didn't think I was being used. And he was nice to me. He cared. Finn liked the same things I did, and to me, these things make for a pretty good friend.

"So we know he's not a Roxdale Charter nub."

"Nope, he's normal." Marilyn and I were walking from fifth period to the library. It was the end of the first Monday of the year, and we were both in a mental state of numbness.

"You gonna call him?"

"I didn't get his number. I might ask my mom to hook us up again sometime. Maybe."

We strolled through an isle of school-approved romance novels and pulled two spinny-chairs up to a computer at the end of the room.

"Wanna help with my Civics project?" I asked.

"A project? Already? Screw it, I'm going on Facebook." The mouse was ripped out of my hand, and before I knew it, I had dozens of life updates from whiny teenagers before my eyes.

As Marilyn checked her notifications, I came up with about seven-hundred reasons in my mind why I hated Facebook. Then Marilyn paused.

"Wait... what did you say his name was?"

"Finn Leighton..." And with that response, she began furiously typing and clicking about the database. "Oh, Marilyn, no!" But I was too late.

"Aha! Finn Leighton, Roxdale Charter High, lives in Springs, fifteen years old... It's crazy what people put online, right?"

"I'll tell you what's crazy: that you're stalking him."

"We're stalking him. Hmmm... He doesn't seem to get online much... His last post was in May." This wasn't a very significant statement; Marilyn was a Facebook addict. "Whoa, ex alert!"

I instinctively leaned over. "Who?"

"Let's see..." She clicked on said ex and brought up the wall of a teenage girl who, well, looked like a prostitute, and whose picture showed herself bent forward, giving the camera the finger. "Whoa..." Marilyn proceeded to read, "Helena Iluvyou Miller, West Springs High—our rivals, how appropriate—, Springs, sixteen... and oh!" Marilyn began cackling so loud I thought the librarian might have a heart attack. Since hiding a body was not on my to-do list, I shushed Marilyn and asked what was so funny. Between giggles, she teased, "Birthday: 6/6/96. She's a devil!" Marilyn went on scrolling. "Yeah, judging from these posts, you've gotta up your inner skank, Red."

"When does it say they ended it?"

"Uh, says about eight months ago."

"Not to be a Peppy Polly, but she doesn't seem like his type, anyway. Honestly, I'm not threatened."

"Just you wait, Red. Just you wait."

I stole the mouse, closed out of the tab, and started on my project.

My next few weeks were spent thrown into my schoolwork, but always at the back of my mind was Finn. I thought about him as a friend. I thought about him as more. I thought about Helena, and I thought about Finn some more. I thought about me, and whether or not I was ready. Would Finn be worth putting my heart out on the line again, or would the finally-closed wound of my past end up open and exposed once more? I couldn't do that again. I didn't want to risk another love infection.

To take my mind off things, I watched T.V., I read books, and I walked around town. Things were different, though. Everything oozed romance. The insanely potent, bittersweet stench seemed to rise out of everything I passed. Every word I saw that started with an "F"—which was a lot, especially when I was walking around certain parts of downtown Springs—seemed at first to say "Finn." Suddenly our conversations played through my head. I heard him agree to share a cheesecake and talk about music and writing, and every time this happened I felt strangely at peace. At this point I would never go as far as to say that I loved him, but he wasn't leaving my mind, and my heart screamed for the smallest share.

It had been almost a month since the night we had dinner at Arlecchino's, and I realized I couldn't focus on anything at all in my life because Finn took up so much of my thoughts. Asking my mom to hook us up again would be admitting defeat, surrendering my argument against her setting me up on a blind date. But I just had to know. I had to know if for once a guy would stand to be around me. He would really want to be with me, and not just to get someone else back.

When I asked my mom if she could get me Finn's phone number—a request which she was all too eager to fulfill—it only took until the end of the day for the seven digits to end up in my hand. I held the notecard-sized slip of paper between my fingers and gazed at the number that I knew had the capability of changing things for me. I picked up my phone off my bedside table, but found myself unable to make the call. I set the paper inside my jacket pocket and plugged my phone in for the night. Maybe tomorrow I would have the guts.

"Well?" Marilyn encouraged somewhat agitatedly.

"I can't just... call him." We walked somewhat lackadaisically, as teenage girls tend to do, through the school parking lot after a long day of school.

"Why not? You have his number."

"He probably doesn't even remember me," I lamented. It was true. It had been over a month and school and friends had probably blotted out his memory of little ole me. Still, what could it hurt...

"Look, I gotta go. Doctor appointment." Marilyn turned to me as she fished for her keys in her bag. "Just promise me, Red, that you'll call him tonight."

I hesitated, but knew she wouldn't leave until I agreed. "Fine. I'll tell you all about it tomorrow."

"That's my girl." She waved goodbye and hopped into her truck.

I walked through the threshold and set down my backpack by the door.

"Raquel," my mom called. Her voice sounded tired, sullen.

"Yeah?" I answered as I entered the kitchen.

"Raquel, honey, I need to tell you something." Her face was almost more pallid than mine, which I didn't think was possible.

"Wait," I said. "I need to make a phone call."

After some hesitation, she said, "Sure honey. Who are you talking to?"

The overuse of the term 'honey' was starting to make me curious, but I continued anyway. "Finn. It's just that I had a pretty good time that night, and I kinda wanted to see if he wanted to hang out again." As soon as the words left my mouth, I was sure that that was what I wanted. I didn't care about anything that had happened, or anything that could happen, just what might happen- what I wanted to happen.

My mother walked slowly over to me and put her hand on my shoulder. I thought I saw a tear well up in her eye. "I talked to Mrs. Leighton today. Finn has just been diagnosed with leukemia."

Chapter 5

My heart stopped just long enough to shatter and crash onto the floor. "Leukemia?" I repeated through numb lips. My mom hugged me. She seemed at an equal loss of words as I was.

"Raquel, honey, I'm... I'm so-"

I felt all the blood rush from my face, but it looked no whiter. I didn't know what could be said or done to make anything any better. So I left. I turned and went up to my room, almost trembling, but not having the resolve to do so. Staring into thin air as if to search for a reason, I closed the door behind me and stood there. Eventually I blinked, gave a shaky sigh, and went to sleep in my cold bed.

For a month and a half afterward, I was frozen in a pensive state. I knew it was right to see him, to meet with him in a sedentary setting, to comfort him when he needed it most. But we only met one time. Finn probably regarded me as just another face, associated me with small-talk conversations, sealed with a cheesecake. For some reason, it was me who couldn't let go. My most prominent flaw—well, my most prominent emotional flaw—was that I love, get crushed, turn to ice, melt once more, then fall apart again with hardly any visible transition. But this wasn't love. It was just a brief infatuation.

Marilyn wouldn't let me live it down. It's not like she rubbed it in my face every chance she got; that wouldn't be being a friend. But every time he came up in conversation, she would give me a look that said, "Hey now. You know you need to see him. Soon."

One Saturday afternoon, we met up for lunch at a diner not too far from school. While we waited on our grilled cheeses, I noticed Marilyn looking down at her fingers, tapping her foot against the metal edge of the chair bottom. She had her thinking face on.

I turned to her with a serious expression meant to coax her into spilling her thoughts. "Okay, what's going on?"

She looked up at me, slightly startled, but clearly knowing what I was getting at. "Oh, well we have that Civics test on Monday."

My face relaxed into a skeptical glare. "You know what I mean. You're thinking about something. Go ahead, say it."

Marilyn gave a short sigh and turned herself toward me. The look in her eyes said that this was something I would really need to listen to, no matter how hard it was to accept. "Red, come on," she started. "This is a serious thing; this is happening. You have a friend in the hospital, and you refuse to see him."

The woman behind the counter slid our plates in front of us and told us to enjoy our meal. I took a bite of my sandwich in an effort to show Marilyn that I didn't want to hear what she had to say.

"I know you don't think you need this," she continued, "but think about it. Imagine if it was me."

This thought made my grilled cheese threaten to make a reappearance. I couldn't imagine Marilyn being in such a position- so sick, trying hard to survive like the trooper I know she is. And what kind of friend would I be if I never once showed my face to let her know I care? We've been best friends since the third grade. No amount of fear or uncertainty of words would prevent me from going to visit her every day. Our friendship just wouldn't die out like that. But that was the thing: I'd met Finn once. How could Marilyn compare our friendship to my one-time meeting with Finn? It wasn't at all the same. Or maybe she saw something in the way I talked about him that led her to believe we could be something...

"Just think about it, Red. What kind of friend will you be?"

Chapter 6

Mom would give me updates about twice a week, telling me how he was doing, how treatment was going. I never knew what I could say. I would just nod and carry on with my day.

Growing up, every day felt like I was suffering. I was ostracized, criticized, and confused. Why did I need to be so different? I felt pain. But I knew now that my pain and suffering could never compare to Finn's. I wanted to tell him how sorry I felt, but I wouldn't know how.

For three more weeks, I thought it over. Should I go see him and tell him that I wanted to see him more, or should I not risk saying something that, based on past experience, I'd inevitably come to regret? After spending my mornings, afternoons, and nights reliving the one night I felt happy and safe with a guy, the night at Arlecchino's, I had made up my mind.

It was Saturday morning and I knew my mom was probably in bed reading. I took a deep breath to hold back any tears bound to come. Upon opening the door, I saw her laying there, reading glasses on, nose in a novel.

"Hey, mom?" I started, hesitating.

"Yeah, hun?"

"I was wondering if you could take me somewhere."

With this, she slipped the reading glasses off her face and turned her full attention over to me. "Sure, got somewhere in mind?"

"Can you take me to the hospital? I want to visit Finn."

The whole way there, I was shaking. But I was also very excited on the inside. The closer we got to the hospital, the happier I felt and the more I couldn't wait to see him, to talk to him again.

When we arrived, mom told me she'd wait out in the car and I promised to come right out when I was done. I made my way through the brisk winter breeze toward the entrance to the Springs Community Hospital. At the visitors desk I was told by a large, tired-looking nurse that I could find him in room A114, east wing. Deep breaths were necessary on my way to A114, but my need to be with him grew stronger every step of the way.

Outside A114, I stopped. This was the room. With a pounding heart, I knocked on the door and entered. Confusion took hold of me when I found myself in a clean, white room with a nurse cleaning up and no one in the bed.

"Where's Finn?" The words slipped right out of my mouth.

"Sweetheart, he's not here anymore," the nurse replied.

"He was discharged?"

Her face was grim. She sighed, patted my shoulder, and left me to myself in the room.

Chapter 7

I simply couldn't fall asleep that night. Knowing that I had put off seeing him until it was too late made me sick in my heart in a way that I thought would surely kill me. Visions of his charming face, his lively smile, that freckle on the side of his cheek danced before my eyes as if trying to tease me and comfort me all at once. At least twice, I could have sworn I felt his strong-yet-soft arms around me before I fell asleep. This time, instead of diving too fast into it, I hadn't dove in fast enough.

In the days that followed, mom told me his funeral would be on Sunday the ninth, and left it up to me to decide whether I wanted to go or not. To me the choice was clear. The past couple months had been filled with me waiting, not making any action. And look where it got me. I had to go to that funeral. I hoped with all my shattered heart that it would bring me some sort of sense of closure.

That day I wore the dress my mom had made me wear on the date. I felt I owed that much to Finn. My hair was up in a bun, the way it had been, but I wore less makeup and a winter jacket this time. I was ready to say goodbye for real.

On our way out to the car, I stared into the thick of trees surrounding our house. I allowed myself to feel the cool air on my skin. I let it cradle me, let it comfort me, let it bring me somewhere safe. I opened the car door and slid into the passenger seat. My mom put the keys in the ignition, then sat back in her seat. She looked at me to see if I was going to be okay.

"You ready?" She asked, putting her hand on my shoulder for reassurance.

"I..." I hadn't the smallest clue how to handle something so... new. So real. "I think so."

Mom turned to face forward and gently placed her hands on the wheel. She moved her foot to the accelerator, then stopped. Her hands slid down to rest at the bottom of the wheel. She bit her lip as if to think carefully of what she was about to say, then turned to me once more.

"It gets better," she started. I turned to her with a blank stare. She tried a different approach. "People come into your life for a reason." She sighed, and stared ahead into the trees. "Your father... he wasn't ever meant to stay in my life. He just wasn't right." There was a pause. I could tell that her mind was conjuring up bittersweet memories, for which I felt somehow guilty. "But Raquel, if he had never been in my life, I would have never had you. And then my life would never have been so great." She smiled a sweet sort of smile and fixed a flyaway hair from my bun. I looked at her reassuringly to let her know how much I appreciated all she was doing for me: taking me to the funeral, talking me through things. After a moment of empty silence, she began backing out of the driveway.

The funeral was at his house, and when I got there friends, family, and neighbors were gathered out in the yard, sharing how they knew him and why they felt he didn't deserve such a premature death. Since I didn't go to Roxdale Charter, and I didn't know a single person there, I made my way over to where a modest shrine had been set up by the garden. Amongst flowers and candles were photos of Finn going through life as a normal, all-American boy. I learned so much more about him just from pictures of him with family, him at his elementary school graduation, him with a fish he caught at the lake, and him at the piano, singing so intently he didn't notice he was having his picture taken.

My eyes landed on a picture of him smiling. Just him smiling. And for a second he became real. I didn't realize how pathetic I looked, smiling back, until a voice ripped me out of my trance.

"Having fun there?" a condescending voice growled from behind me.

I whirled around to see a girl about my age with heavy eyeliner, poorly dyed red hair, and a distractingly low-cut shirt staring at me expectantly.

"Yo, got a problem?" she hissed.

"Uh, sorry, I'm Red Reeves. I go to East Springs." I wasn't quite sure what else to say, so I stuck my hand out in front of me for her to shake.

"Helena Miller," she said after an uncomfortable pause. Introducing myself with the name of her school's rival may not have been the best move. "How'd you know Finn?" I could tell she was the jealous type.

"Oh, I really only met him briefly. It's a funny story, actually. Our parents sort of set us up on a blind-"

"I'm his girlfriend." She sneered.

At this point, another teenage girl passed by and said, "Ex-girlfriend, Helena." She turned to me. "Since May." With this, she walked away.

"Doesn't matter," Helena carried on. "We were on-and-off, anyway."

I sort of pitied her. She had just as much of an opportunity as I did to reconnect with Finn, and she probably had less desire to. But now that she knew she could never have him, she figured no one else could.

Helena sized me up one last time, then said, "Later," and turned back to her friends. For the next ten minutes or so, from time to time I would flicker my eyes over to Helena and her posse only to see her staring at me, but consumed in conversation. If I listened, I could make out words such as "freak," "home wrecker," and "tacky." Eventually I stopped listening because I figured everything else would be just as hypocritical.

A while later, a woman I figured to be Mrs. Leighton, Finn's mother, asked for everyone's attention so that she could say a few words. It took every fiber of everyone's beings not to spill over with tears when she described his life and personality, but nothing could stop the crying. According to Mrs. Leighton, Finn had both a brain and a soul worth sharing with the world, and stopped to help whomever he could. It all sounded so cliché, but I believed it. He did seem like that sort of person. She talked about his involvement with extracurriculars, and all of his special talents. Then she shared with us something that opened a window which would take some time and serious perseverance for me to close.

"Finn liked to write. I remember he would lock himself in his room for hours, just so he could be by himself, and he would write. At the hospital during treatment, he asked for a pen and paper, and he spent most of his free time writing things that I wasn't allowed to read until after he went home. Well, he's home now. So there is something he wrote just before he passed that I would like to share with you:

Someplace Else

Through the voices, noise, and smell, I can tell her mind is someplace else.
I'm caught up in her unreadable face, while she is just caught up in space.
I'll try to bring her down to earth, but talk to her way up there first.
I'll tell her all the things I've dreamed of telling her, and then we'll lean
Into a new dream I've longed to live, and then go back. Oh, only if..."

Through sniffles and tears, everyone clapped. Mrs. Leighton became too emotional at this point to carry on talking, so Finn's poem wrapped up the speech. Not a minute later, Helena approached me. This time, a smug smile graced her face.

"Huh, guess he really did love me." She poured herself some water from the refreshment table next to me, spotted an attractive cousin of Finn's, gave a coquettish glance in his direction, and unbuttoned her shirt one more notch.

"Uh, I thought he dumped you months ago," I rebutted. I guess I must have rained on her parade pretty bad, for her entire demeanor hardened.

"It was mutual. And come on. He wouldn't leave this and not come running back. No one does." She sipped her water, still watching me out of the corner of her eye.

"It's just that we had just gone out not too long before he wrote that, and-"

"If you think for one second he wrote that about you, you are sadly mistaken," she snapped. "Watch your back." And with that, she left me to enjoy the rest of the funeral.

Chapter 8

Helena was mean. She was skanky, she was jealous, she was cocky- in more ways than one- and she had my mind in a knot. Could it be possible that in his last few days, it was her he was proclaiming his love for? Or was it possible that maybe he felt the same connection that I had finally decided to pursue? Flipping through all the possibilities in my head would solve nothing.

"So you met Helena?" Marilyn asked between classes.

"Yeah," I answered with a sigh.

"Was she... nice?"

"Oh yeah, she was a ball of sunshine! She baked me cookies, then pooped out flowers for me!"

"Hey now, no need to get snippy."

"She's so not over Finn." I lowered my voice and told her, "His mom read a poem that he wrote just before he-" I had to pause to stop myself from tearing up. Marilyn gave me a reassuring hug. I continued, "It was about a girl. A girl he really liked. But Helena made it very clear that it was about her. But I really don't think so."

Marilyn suddenly had a pensive look on her face. "You said he wrote a lot?"

"Yeah."

"So he probably kept all his stuff in one place, like a notebook, maybe?"

"You're saying I should ask his mother, whose son just died of leukemia last week, if I can pry through his stuff?" I retorted.

Suddenly Marilyn boasted a smug smile. "That's exactly what I'm saying."

That night, pulling into Finn's neighborhood, the reality of the situation hit me. It was kind of terrible how I was taking advantage of a grieving mother. But I had to prove Helena wrong. Not just for the sake of being right, but for the sake of being at peace.

"Which one is it?" Being best friends with one of the few licensed drivers in the tenth grade had its advantages. My mom would never have taken me here if she had known my motives. But Marilyn was all for helping me find the truth.

"Uh, third one on the right, I believe." And indeed, we reached the house that hosted the funeral: Finn's house. "Okay, wish me luck. I'll be right back, hopefully with the book, or whatever it is."

"Go get 'em, tiger."

I gave a sweet smile and headed toward the door, instinctively hugging myself for reassurance.

It took no more than a few seconds after the first doorbell ring for Mrs. Leighton to shuffle over and greet me. After briefly talking about the weather, I stated my cause, holding back any hesitation that would annul the purpose of my trip.

"That was a beautiful poem that you read at the funeral. Finn wrote that?"

Mrs. Leighton, with her tired eyes and shaking composure, answered, "Yes. My son was very talented. He got into the typical teenage-boy trouble, but he was going to go places." I could tell that she was heartbroken and longed to hold her son one more time. This made my request that much harder.

"He was. So... is there a place... some sort of notebook, maybe, where he kept the things he wrote?"

"Ah, yes," she smiled, her eyes somewhere else. "He was so protective over that thing. Made me wonder if he had written where to find a body or some nonsense!" She let out a giggle, and then a tear.

"I'm... I'm very sorry, Mrs. Leighton." I paused before I asked, "Do you think I could maybe... see it?"

She stared at me with empty eyes until she said, "Of course not." She smiled as sweetly as she could. "And why do you want so badly to read my son's private things?"

"I'm very sorry. I don't mean to pry, it's just that I had a lot of fun on our date, and I was curious to get to know him better."

"Well, it's too late now. These old poems and stories aren't him, sweetie. And they don't belong to you."

I wanted so badly to explain to her what they would mean to me, and how necessary they were in me finding my own closure. But she wouldn't hear it.

"It's a school night. You better be getting home, dear." She sniffed and closed the door.

I had told Marilyn everything Finn's mom had said as we drove home. Marilyn assured me that it was nothing personal, that she was still grieving. But that didn't help console me in the least.

"Does it really mean that much to you, to know whether or not he felt the same?" she asked me.

"I'd really like to know. I mean, I've never had such a connection with a guy in one night. I didn't feel shut out, and I didn't feel criticized. I want to know if it was real."

"Then we're getting that book."

"How? His mom almost flipped when I asked for it!"

She gave me an intent look as she parked in my driveway. "You prepared to break some rules?"

Chapter 9

Friday we had off school. But mom didn't have off work, which meant that neither did Mrs. Leighton. So her house would be empty for at least half an hour. And that was all the time I needed.

At twelve sharp, our plan would go into action. Marilyn would drive me to Finn's house, and I would open the front door with the key kept underneath the blue flowerpot on the porch. Marilyn had done some research and it turned out that one of Finn's friends had posted on Facebook a recollection of the time he used that key to come see him when he was sick with the flu. This gave us the location of the key, so from there it was pretty straightforward. I would go upstairs, find the room that seemed most likely to be his, retrieve the book, and get out as fast as I could, locking the door behind me. It seemed flawless, foolproof. And we were about to put it into action.

On the ride there, we went over the plan at least ten times, not passing over a single detail. The flustered butterflies in my gut told me this was not worth proving such a small point. But it was about more than proving it to Helena. It was about proving it to myself.

We pulled into the Leightons' driveway, and I felt shaky but certain. It was go time.

Marilyn wished me luck, and I fearlessly breezed down the walkway to the front porch. I had never done anything so... illegal... but instead of thinking, I lifted the pretty blue flowerpot that housed a single tulip, just beginning to wither away for the season.

Nothing was underneath.

A hot wave of panic flushed over me. I checked the underside of the pot, looked under all the other pots and inside them, but to no avail. I didn't come all this way for nothing. There must be a key somewhere. My breaths grew shakier and I almost turned back, when I noticed a small, blue hanging pot hovering just above the corner of the porch. There was tape on the underside. I folded the tape back, and along with a narrow stream of potting soil, down fell something shiny. It was the key.

With hardly any trouble, I opened the door and stepped inside, closing it behind me. It was a beautiful house- contemporary, yet classically warm and inviting. But I was on a mission. Most teenage boys' bedrooms are located on the second floor, so I started there. The sun filled the upstairs hallway, and the beauty of it calmed my pounding heart somewhat. In my childhood, when I had fantasized about going on a super-secret, illegal mission, I expected the scenery to be less... welcoming. I felt at home.

With no time to spare, I cracked open every door I passed by and peeked in, until I came to a room with white walls and a teenage-boy-looking leather recliner in my view. I opened the door wider to reveal that it was, indeed, a bedroom—it had a bed and closet with a backpack thrown down next to it—but something else made me very lightheaded and perplexed.

On the wall above the bed was a Justin Bieber poster. Maybe Finn hadn't written that poem for me or Helena.

Then I caught sight of the trashcan. It was pink and said "Liz" on it in curly letters. This was Finn's sister's room; his must be farther on.

I moved along, and the next door down was, upon first glance, unmistakably Finn's room. The centerpiece of the space was a small, not-so-grand piano, but it looked beautiful and like something he would play. The posters all around the walls were of the artists and people who, he had said at dinner, inspired him. I smiled beyond my previously known capability of smiling when I noticed a poster that featured a cheesecake meme. This was Finn's room, and his little journal had to be somewhere in there.

I looked through the books and papers in the bookcase, and used a crazy amount of will power not to spend any time looking through his yearbooks. I didn't want to be a stalker; I was there for a specific reason... to pry through his most personal belonging that held his feelings and thoughts. Yeah, never mind. I know what it looks like.

I checked through his backpack, his closet, under his bed- and nothing. His mom probably hadn't touched his room since he got sick. And here I was, rummaging through it like there was no tomorrow, which there wouldn't be if I came out empty-handed. This thought made me very frustrated. I looked in the trashcan and shouted "Hellooo, journal? You in there?" A deranged fury broke loose and swept over me. I lifted up the top of the piano. "Hellooo?" But before I closed it, something caught my eye. I peered inside again and, sure enough, there was a small, blue rectangle hiding in a crevice.

I reached my arm as far in as it could possibly go, running on pure adrenaline just to feel around for it. And then I came back up with the book in my hand. I flipped through it, and sure enough, it was filled with chicken scratch of poems, songs, sheet music, and stories. The book was no larger than my hand and not very thick. But it was dense with Finn, and that was all that mattered to me.

A wave of victory swept over me, a long-missed sensation. Then the front door opened downstairs. My heart stopped as footsteps echoed around the house. Marilyn must have come inside to check on me.

Without thinking, I shouted, "Marilyn, is that you?"

The footsteps stopped. "Who's there? Who's in this house?" It was Mrs. Leighton's voice.

Chapter 10

Panic rose in my throat. How could I be so reckless? My first time attempting anything sneaky and I blew it. No, it wasn't too late. It couldn't be. There had to be some way out—an escape.

I didn't come all this way for nothing. I tucked the notebook into my jacket pocket and bolted out of that room. But I stopped short when I reached the end of the hall and looked out the window. It was a good way down with nothing to break my fall, if I could get the window open before Mrs. Leighton reached me. At this point, tears welled up in my eyes, and the back of my throat tightened.

"I'm calling the police!" she yelled from downstairs. Maybe there was a back door somewhere down there. I knew that any way this ended, I must know the truth. It would kill me if Finn loved and craved Helena in his final moments, but it would be worlds more painful to not be able to move forward with my life, plagued by uncertainty.

I swallowed hard and crept down the stairs, all but praying that they weren't the squeaky kind. I hadn't noticed on my way up if they were. My feet shook as they hit each step. I could hear, over the pounding of blood in my head, Mrs. Leighton on the phone with the police, describing a female voice in her house. How could I have mistaken the time she would be home? Maybe they let her off early because she was going through so much.

Upon reaching the bottom of the stairs, I realized that the front door was only a few feet from where I stood. Suddenly a flush of hope came over me. I took Finn's notebook out of my jacket pocket and rubbed my fingers across it for reassurance. There was only time enough for me to slip it back in before my wrists were seized by the trembling hands of a distraught mother.

At the police station, I waited in an uncomfortable metal chair in the corner of a large room while Mrs. Leighton seemed to be frantically explaining the situation to an officer. I waited for over half an hour, taking deep, measured breaths. I felt scared, but mostly betrayed. Pulling away from Finn's house in the police car,

I had noticed that Marilyn's car was no longer parked in the driveway. She had ditched me. My brain struggled to make sense of the situation when my mom shuffled into the station.

She spotted me, and immediately made a beeline toward my lonely corner. She was still in her work clothes, although her hair had begun to fall out of its neat little up-do. "Oh, Raquel, are you all right? They called me and told me that you had... oh, what is going on here?"

"I'll tell you what's going on!" Mrs. Leighton interjected. The situation was explained to my mother, a confused, breathless, nervous wreck. After the completely true, yet exaggerated story was told, my mom turned to me.

"And what on earth would drive you to do such a thing, Raquel?" I was dumbfounded, speechless. There was no excuse other than the truth. I was never an actress, or remotely successful liar. So what else could I say?

"I just... I just wanted this..." I mustered, and pulled the notebook out from my jacket pocket. Before I had time to make eye contact with anyone, it was snatched out of my hand in a wild huff.

"I told you once, young lady, and you should learn to respect your elders' wishes! I told you that this does not belong to you!" A certain possessive edge crept into Mrs. Leighton's voice, as if it were not the notebook, but Finn himself who could not be mine. Mrs. Leighton turned to my mother and stated flatly, "Please do learn to control your daughter." With that, she thanked the officer and marched out of the room, notebook in tow.

"We are going to have a long talk later, young lady." And that was all my mother had to say to me for the rest of the day.

Chapter 11

My mood was remorseful the next Monday, until I caught sight of her blue hair feather in the hallway. Then it changed to furious. When I reached Marilyn, I nearly broke her arm, shoving her up against her locker.

"Hey, what was that-" Marilyn whirled around to see me staring at her, expecting an explanation or something, something that might remotely make up for her ditching me on our super-secret, super-illegal mission. "Oh, Red, Red, I'm so-"

"What happened?" My voice was low. I didn't want to be as mean as I had been by pushing her. Marilyn, my best friend, best confidant, and only person I could trust when the world started to turn on me. Why she would do this, I didn't know.

"I texted you! To let you know she was coming! I told you to meet me three doors down... I couldn't just be sitting in the driveway, you know that! Oh, Red, I'm so sorry. I swear I waited for you 'till I saw the cops take you away. Speaking of which-" The full impact of her rapid-fire apology hit me like a ton of bricks. My phone. I threw my arms around Marilyn, regretting all the negative thoughts I had held against her, regretting shoving her into her locker.

"Oh, Marilyn, I'm so sorry. I guess I was so freaked out and busy looking for the notebook I didn't feel my phone buzz. I believe you. My mom took my phone away afterwards." Honestly, I felt bad for doubting her.

"That's fine, as long as you're safe and sound and not in juvie," she joked. "But did you get the notebook?"

I thought about that little notebook. Suddenly it was so small in my memory. It was such a tiny physical object resembling something so big. It was a life, Finn's life, or the closest thing I had to it. It struck me as funny in that moment that I had allowed something so small to be so critical to my sanity, or to drive a barrier between me and my best friend. "Yeah, but she took it away before I got to look at it."

Marilyn gave a sympathetic sigh. "Well, Red, just know that no matter what Helena says, the guy you say Finn was would never go back to her in his last days."

I knew she was right, but still, I couldn't help feeling uncertain. That notebook was my key to knowing whether I could ever be worth it to a guy, a quality guy who didn't need me to get anyone else. I would have to be confident that someone would come along who would care for me no matter what had happened in the past... no matter what Finn may or may not have felt for me.

Without confirmation from Finn's writing, I started to force myself to feel closure throughout the day, although that's not really an easy task for anyone. When I got home, I knew the only thing to do was to throw myself into my homework, just as mom did with her work.

I didn't think much of it when the doorbell rang. Then my mom called me downstairs, saying it was for me. On my way down, I expected to see Marilyn. But I almost tripped when I saw Mrs. Leighton standing in the doorway, staring sullenly at me. I pushed myself to make my way over to her, combing over in my head what she could possibly want. Maybe she expected a lengthier apology.

"I'll leave you two ladies," My mom said awkwardly, and she was gone. We stood there for a moment, each waiting for the other to say something. I figured I'd be the one to break the silence.

"Hello, Mrs. Leighton," I started. Before I could start my apology, she reached into her purse and began digging around.

"I figured..." She pulled her hand out of the purse, "that you should have this." In her extended hand, placed for me to take, was none other than Finn's notebook.

"But-"

"Please. You obviously cared for my boy. I think that you..." Tears began to roll down her pale cheeks. "Just take it, please. I don't mind that you read it, just please don't throw it away or lose it or anything..." I could tell that this blue rectangle of chicken scratch was this woman's last connection to her son. It was almost too precious for me to take. But I had worked so hard for it, and I still needed an answer. It didn't matter, anyway; before I could say anything more, the book was in my hand, and Mrs. Leighton was gone.

Chapter 12

I stood, dumbfounded, by the front door. My arm was almost shaking; I could feel the foreign object sitting in my palm. I tossed it over in my hands after closing the door, flipping through the pages, feeling its essence. Is this what I wanted? Is this what I had fought for, almost turned against my best friend for? It was absolutely what I wanted, though it was nothing to fight over. This notebook was not a trophy, it was answers. It was closure in something that was not a game, but a tragedy. And I craved the words of solace I knew it had to offer.

In my room, I flipped through the pages of Finn. There were songs and poems that were hardly legible, and I struggled to make out every fourth word. Still, their power was just as strong and effective. There were passages about sports with dad, trips to the lake, and all the other small things that ordinary people wouldn't find noteworthy. But that was the thing: Finn wasn't ordinary. It was clear by reading his precious collection that he had a beautiful mind, one that I regretted not getting to know better.

An unmistakable word caught my eye toward the back of the book.

Cheesecake.

I read it over a few times to make sure that was what it really said. And indeed, the poem it belonged to was an unmistakable account of our date. He described me as a sort of angel, and I'm not just flattering myself. The end of the piece was wishes to see this girl again. The rest of the poems and other pieces- his last- were about his illness and me. They were unmistakably about me. Some mentioned specific details from our date, and others, I just knew. My satisfaction came partly from proving Helena Miller wrong, but mostly from knowing I'd been marked as beautiful. Not just in a great guy's mind, but in his journal of his thoughts. It was on paper that I had hope. My chance with Finn was obviously gone, but I knew there was a reason to keep my chin up. I'm young, after all, and there's still plenty of time.

The birds in the park in downtown Springs were few at this time of year, but they sang relentlessly. Marilyn and I lay back-to-back on the gum-laden public bench, staring into the trees around us.

"Helena was wrong after all, huh?" Marilyn concluded after I told her of my findings.

"Guess so," was all I could get out. A peaceful pause hung in the air for a moment.

"You happy?" she asked. I had to think about that. Of course, if I could have chosen the outcome of things, this wouldn't be it. Finn would be alive. But I couldn't help that sort of thing.

"As happy as I can be," I sighed.

A piercing shriek of laughter snapped us to attention. We turned our heads in the direction of the sound, to see Helena and her little posse moseying along the pathway next to us. Upon spotting us, a sneer was shot in our direction.

"Well, well." A tight pseudo-smile crossed Helena's face. "What have we here?" she said, slightly wobbly, in fact, almost falling over. Drugs were probably overwhelming her system.

"Oh," said Marilyn with a sudden condescending brightness to her voice. "Apparently, the girl Finn actually wanted to be with!"

Helena turned as best she could without falling to the group of ditsy teenage girls behind her, who were giving us patronizing looks, though they probably didn't even know why. "What are you talking about?" she retorted, turning her attention back to us. Suddenly, I knew something had to be set straight.

"His mom let me read his notebook. His last poems... they were about me."

"Ha, how do you know that?"

"Tell me, did he ever split a cheesecake with you on a date? Did he tell you his hopes and dreams and love the way your red eyes glowed 'so warmly?' Did he-" Suddenly a desire to win took over me as I described the things Finn wrote about me. "Because that's what he wrote in his last weeks. It was me he was thinking of."

"You're lying," Helena sneered. But I could hear the edge of fear in her voice. I could see in her eyes how badly she needed to believe that he still had feelings for her. Because underneath her vicious, snake-like exterior, Helena was weak. She knew how fake and hollow she was, and believing

Finn still cared, that was the only thing keeping her going. Suddenly, our little game seemed juvenile. I took a long pause.

"Yeah, yeah I am." I could practically taste Marilyn's confusion and disapproval boring into my skin. But whatever. Helena needed this.

"Of course you are." Her façade was slowly failing, but she maintained her composure as she crudely dismissed herself, leading her posse alongside her.

I knew that in time Marilyn would understand, and she did. There was no competition to be won, just confidence to be gained. Sitting in peaceful silence on that park bench, I realized that every girl deserves to feel pretty, just not at anyone else's expense. As I got older and moved on, that night with Finn got revoked from its status as best night of my life, but it always remained special to me. I lived with an open heart, because no matter what the impending consequences, giving it a chance is the first step to anything working out. Don't wait for happiness to just come, seize it, and give yourself reason to believe.

Believers Dream Publishing

Where Teens Can Realize Their Dreams

A small publisher dedicated to publishing books for teens written by teens.

www.believersdreampublishing.com

www.ingramcontent.com/pod-product-compliance
Lightning Source LLC
Chambersburg PA
CBHW050502110726
47899CB00003B/1039